For my family,

Fred, Roman and Manny

Tales from the Amazon

ADAPTED BY
MARTIN ELBL and **J. T. WINIK**

ILLUSTRATED BY
GERDA NEUBACHER

Designed by
J. T. WINIK

Cover Design
PATRICIA NOVAK

Separations and Film
LITHO COLOR SERVICES LTD.
Mississauga, Ontario

Copyright 1986 by Hayes Publishing Ltd.
Burlington, Ontario

ISBN 0-88625-127-3

Printed in Hong Kong

Hayes Publishing Ltd., 3312 Mainway, Burlington, Ontario L7M 1A7, Canada

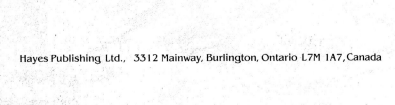

The Man Who Married a Star

On a rich, green bank of the Muddy River there once lived a young hunter. In spite of his youth, he was renowned for his bravery. No man past or present could match the accuracy of his bow. Jaguar pelts in plenty adorned his house, and his huntsman's necklace of teeth and claws wound more than five times around his neck. Even the rich merchants from the far-off lands near the Western Mountains traveled great distances, on foot and by river, to barter silver and turquoise for his precious furs.

The young hunter's tribe, the brave Chamacocos, took great pride in his fame, and there was not a single girl who would not gladly have become his wife. But in vain they cooked sweet porridge for him. Their smiles were wasted on the young man who preferred to live alone, only with his dear sister, Flower. And so it was that he enjoyed well his youth, riches and glory.

3

One day, very suddenly, he began to sicken and wilt. His face grew pale and his eyes lifeless. More and more often he left the merry company of his young friends and set forth on long and lonely hunting expeditions, taking only his dogs. Always he returned burdened with magnificent prey, but sadder and sulkier each time.

"Tell me, what's happened to you, oh pride of the tribe?" asked the old chief Apochangra. "You seem like a shadow from the realm of the dead! You do not eat. You are no longer joyful. Which one of the sorcerers has stolen your happiness? What sore illness weighs you down?"

"No illness, wise Apochangra," answered the young hunter. "Do not ask what ails me for there is no hope. If I told you the true cause of my grief, you would think that I've gone out of my mind."

"You should not speak so, my boy," said Apochangra. "There is no trouble so great that some remedy cannot be found to heal it. Only tell me, what is that dark stone on your heart?"

"Look to the black sky, O Venerable One," said the hunter. "Do you see that beautiful silver star?"

The old chief nodded, for without a doubt, one star stood out from all the rest.

"Yes," said the hunter. "It is that one and no other. Only that star spreads such great light all around. No other is so beautiful. For the sake of her my peace is gone. I love her, my chief, and there is nothing I desire more than to marry her."

"What kind of words do I hear?" lamented Apochongra. "Who ever heard of such a thing — to have a star for a wife? Has your fame blinded you? Are not the earthly girls of our own tribe good enough for you?"

From that time on the tribe began to avoid the sad hunter. Only his sister, Flower, remained faithfully by his side, but silently, in secret, she wiped away her tears. Surely, she thought, her brother's soul would soon leave his body and soar upwards to the heavens to join his beloved star.

One night, however, the young hunter fell to rest in a woodland clearing. As he slept, a silver brilliance appeared and grew wide over the tops of the trees. From its rays the most beautiful of maidens descended. She was dressed in robes of silver with strands of starlight woven through her raven-black hair.

"Wake up from your sad dream, O hunter."

"Who are you?" he whispered, but as the words fell from his lips, he knew.

"I am Yohle, the one you so much desire and for whom you have suffered so long. I could look upon your pain no more and so I've come to your earthly region," said the Star Maiden. "I will be your wife if you wish, but there is a difficulty to it."

"I will fight with all the world to win you, if need be!" said the hunter joyously.

"No, no," smiled Yohle. "The problem is that I am a star, a child of the night sky. If I stayed with you, you would have to keep me in darkness during the daylight hours. Thus, I would be your wife only at night, only for half a life. What then will become of your huntsman's fame?"

"What is all fame to me if I have you! I can go hunting at dawn."

"Well then, but what will you do with me when your village packs up and moves to another place, as it does every year?"

"Do not worry, my fair one. I will ask my sister, Flower, to weave a great basket with a tight lid for you. In it you will rest comfortably and sheltered from the sun's rays."

But Yohle had one more request. "It must be kept a secret that I live in your hut," she said. "Only your good sister should ever know of it — no one else!"

Yohle brought only happiness into her husband's house. Flower was light of heart at seeing her brother's joy, and so peacefully flowed the time under the roof of their hut. Star told Flower many secrets and taught her wonders never known on the face of the earth. Never had anyone seen such beautiful embroideries as those that adorned the clothes of the young hunter and his sister. The good Flower, with her new knowledge, went healing illness and disease, all the while singing songs of great joy.

Alas, curiosity and jealousy spoiled the sleep of the other villagers. Their suspicions consumed them like fire.

"Who lives in your house, O Flower?" they asked. "What a strange light shines from your hut at night! Whose silvery voice sings there after the sun has set?"

"Who would live there but my brother and I?" said Flower. The villagers turned away un-soothed, whispering among themselves.

And so it was until one day a most beautiful child was seen at the young hunter's house.

"Whose is that silvery child, Flower?" said the women.

"It is mine! Whose would it be?"

"Do not try to fool us!" hissed the women. "It cannot be yours." They nagged from dawn to sunset, but still Flower told them nothing.

"We must know what secret the hunter keeps hidden in his house," said the chief's wife to the others. "Have you noticed that huge basket which Flower guards by her side every time our village is on the move? She cares for it more than for herself. The secret is most surely to be found inside." And so they made a plan.

11

One day when the hunter was away they wrenched the basket from Flower's keeping. Flower was powerless against the strength of the other women, but in vain did they try to open the lid. Yohle held it firmly from inside.

"Leave me in peace, women!" cried Yohle.

Yohle would not let go of the lid, and so they kindled a great fire under the basket. Suddenly the Star Maiden burst from her abode in the form of a burning thunder flash! Clasping her little son in her arms she soared high into the sky.

When the young hunter returned he was filled with great rage and sadness. When night fell, however, the Star Maiden called down to him.

"Come, my husband, to my starry land. Here, there is no evil and enough wild game for all."

The hunter gathered up his dogs and set forth instantly on his long journey. Most surely he reached the land of stars. Even today we can see him. When the sky is dark with night, look high. There, near his brilliant loved one shines the great hunter. With his bow bent and arrow at the ready, he leads his pack of hunting dogs.

Why The Old Never Grow Young

Once upon a time, when there were as many jaguars in the jungle as there are parrots in the tops of the trees today, a young witch doctor lived in a village not far from the steep Sugar Hill. Veji knew a remedy for any kind of illness, common or uncommon, for, despite his youth, he'd wandered far and wide and had sat at the feet of the most renowned masters of his art. Even the powerful and jealous wizards of the far-off Western Mountains shared their wisdom with him.

Veji also had a kind heart. He did not deny his help to those in need of it, even if there should be no reward for his skills but a good word. "All is well," he replied with a smile to those who were too poor to give him beautiful horses, rare furs and precious jewels. "Others have enough to pay for both you and themselves."

Only against death and old age was he powerless. Famous hunters grew old, tottering and helpless before his very eyes. In vain did Veji try out his cures. In the end, even his father grew old and died, to the unspeakable grief of all.

"This cannot be!" wailed Veji. "There are remedies for so many human ills, there should be one for old age and death too. Only our eyes are to blame, not to see the answer."

In his sorrow he put fire to mounds of costly fragrances, anointed his body and began to dance in order to seek counsel from the gods. For three days he danced without pause, taking neither food nor drink. Finally, the spirit of his dead father appeared to him and spoke.

"If you desire to find a remedy for old age, vainly do you search for it in the teachings of the wizards. Only Onoengrodi, who created men such as they are, can help you. To get your wish you must go to his house and there look for what you are after."

"But where is his house, father? Oh, if only I knew!"

"You must travel many days," said the ghost. "Many nights you will pass under the stars. You will grow weary, but you must not stop until you reach the very end of the world. There, where the sky meets with the earth, is the Great One's house."

"Then will Onoengrodi give me the cure for old age?"

"He will, but you must beware of three things. Do not eat any of his food or you will instantly be changed into a quick-footed deer. Do not smoke any of Onoengrodi's tobacco or you will instantly become a tobacco field. Most importantly, do not look even out of the corner of your eye at Onoengrodi's daughter. If you do, you will fall deeply in love with her and so, never be able to leave her side."

Veji thanked the spirit of his father and set forth on his journey. After many days, he reached the very rim of the world, where all things are enshrouded in gossamer mist and clouds. There, Veji saw the house of the Great One.

"Welcome, Veji!" smiled Onoengrodi. "I know what brings you here and, although your wish is not wise, you will have it. But first, sit and rest. Share with me my feast of tender roast meat for you must be hungry after your travels."

"A thousand times I thank you, Onoengrodi," Veji answered, "but I am much too tired, and my stomach would be too weak to bear so hearty a meal."

"Well spoken, Veji! In that case, smoke a pipe with me. What would people say if I did not offer you anything?"

"Thank you with all my heart, O Great One," Veji replied, "but your tobacco would be too strong for an ordinary man like myself. Let us share my tobacco instead."

"As you wish, Veji. Let us smoke then! Later, my daughter will prepare a bath for you. She will rub your body with a soothing uruku balm, which will refresh you."

But even in that test, Veji held his ground. As he heard Onoengrodi's daughter coming into the room, he closed his eyes firmly and did not open them until she had left.

"Well, you are clever, young sorcerer," said Onoengrodi. "Although it is against the grain of all order, there is nothing I can do but give to you this comb of youth. Whoever you comb with it will become young and strong again."

Veji gave great thanks for the precious gift and set out on his return journey with haste.

He was already quite far from the Great One's house when he heard someone running after him.

"Veji! Veji! Stop!" cried a voice. "You have forgotten your pipe and all of your tobacco in our house!"

"A small matter is that," said Veji as he glanced over one shoulder. "Let Onoengrodi keep it in exchange for his comb."

Alas, one is never too careful. It was Onoengrodi's daughter herself and so beautiful was she that Veji instantly fell in love with her — exactly as his dead father had foretold.

Taking her hand, Veji forgot what he had come for. He forgot his village and all the rest of the world and he followed her back to Onoengrodi's land. If, someday, he should find the strength to return to the land of men, everybody would be forever young and there would be no death. But then, would not the world burst with fullness and crack apart like an overripe fruit of the borracho tree? Indeed, the wise Onoengrodi knows best for us.

The Sun, The Moon and The Rain

Long, long ago, when the world still cried over its milk-teeth — so long ago that even the oldest of great-great-grandfathers would have heard of those days from their own great-great-grandfathers — the Sun, the Moon and the Rain lived among ordinary people. That was on the muddy banks of the river Ibahy, a place long forgotten, where the colorful orchids grew and where parrots flew high above the tree-tops in screeching swarms.

Sun, Moon and Rain had human bodies then and human joys and sorrows also. They laughed a bright laugh and wept salty tears as often as any other mortal, and you couldn't have pointed your finger to say, at first sight: "Here is Sun. And look that's Moon over there, and here is Rain, splashing in a puddle!"

Golden Sun was a handsome young warrior, the strongest of all and the bravest of the brave. His wife, the gentle Morning Star, looked each day into his wondrous eyes with happiness, and it's true, no other had eyes like his. One glance from them was enough to make every grain ripen, and the whole village bathed in the warmth of its glow.

Silver Moon, the Nightly Hunter, knew all the hidden paths which game would tread, and from a merry hunt where he was the leader, no one ever went home with empty hands. When Moon shook out his long silver hair, arrows flew easily into the hearts of prey, borne and guided by the light of his locks.

And Rain?

Old and wise, he lived in a lonely reed hut at the edge of the forest, not very far from the other homes. He took care of brooks and rivers, that they might flow well and full, that sources and springs might never run dry and that all the trees, flowers and animals might receive enough water, without which there is no life.

But, alas, the foolish man is never content, and so it happened that everybody, farmers and hunters alike, began to grumble and complain from morning 'till night. The Sun's rays were too hot, they said, and the Moon's beams let them have no sleep, and all the time they were soaking wet because of that silly old Rain.

One day, hesitant and shuffling their feet — for they were not quite easy at heart with themselves — they approached Golden Sun and asked him to leave.

"Please, Golden Sun, the heat of your eyes suffocates us and causes us to feel tired and lazy. Leave our village please and all will be well between us."

At that, Sun's mind was filled with sadness and his face turned purple with anger. Without a single word of good-bye, he did what they wanted and rose high up into the sky, higher than the top of the highest palm tree.

Too far away now, the Sun's rays were weakened, for he had all the rivers, plains, seas and mountains the world over to shine his light on. The maize furrows and vegetable gardens wilted and turned yellow and, when winter winds blew cold through the walls of their huts, the people grew yet more dissatisfied.

"Nightly Hunter, Silver Moon, leave our village please!" begged the people. "Your silvery brilliance is too bright, and we barely get a wink of sleep. We only lay, tossing about and getting no rest 'till dawn comes again."

For some time the Moon looked at them, speechless, and they looked back, not knowing what to say. Then, cool, disdainful and frowning angrily, Moon strode away along the river bank and soared high to his new home among the stars.

After that, hunters began to return to the village tired and wounded, their hands empty. No more did Moon guide them to their prey, but instead he played jests with their eyes, enchanting them with visions and leading them astray. Without deer to eat, poverty settled in their huts and hunger in their bellies, but even that did not make the people any wiser.

"Old Man Rain, you will have to leave our village," said the people angrily. "We are wet and drenched to the bone because of you! Without the Sun now to dry us and warm us as he used to, we will catch our deaths with cold. Go now, old one, and leave us be!"

"You poor, blind fools," Rain sputtered. "Is your lot not bad enough already, now that you have chased away your Sun and your Moon? Will you have still more trouble? What will you do when all the sources dry up and the Sun's breath begins burning all your crops? Where will you look for me? How will you call me to your aid, then?"

"How should we call you, old one?" laughed the people. "We will call you by your name, of course — Rain! Rain! And now, do not bother us anymore. Be off with you!" Rain shrugged his shoulders and grimaced. In the morning he gathered up all his belongings, put fire to his hut and walked away.

Sun scorched the land without mercy. Moon, the Nightly Hunter, played his game of hide and seek with the hunters and not a drop of rain fell from the azure sky for months on end. Cracks split the earth and the maize crops withered. Streams, once full with gurgling waters, became graves of gray dust, and hunger hollowed the eyes of the villagers. "Rain! O Rain!" cried the people for days on end, but their calls went unheard. At last, the people turned to the Wise One, old Na-ma-ka-ra-ne for help.

Rocking his head like some ageless, dry-skinned turtle, Na-ma-ka-ra-ne sighed. "It is a long time now since Sun and Moon have left us, both of them full of bitter contempt and hate," said the Wise One. "Only if people of their own blood still lived in your village, might they help you, but by the bad way that you have treated them they would not know you as brothers."

"But what are we to do then?" cried the people. "Look, our children are dying!"

The wise old Na-ma-ka-ra-ne thought long and hard, but finally he raised his head to speak. "You who are relatives, however distant, of the Sun, call yourselves the Golden Ones," he said. "And you who are relatives, however distant, of the Moon, know yourselves now as the Moon People. Call yourselves the Silver Ones," he said. "Then all of you will be related to them and Sun and Moon might take pity on you."

"And Rain?" someone dared to ask.

"That is a weightier matter," said Na-ma-ka-ra-ne. "No one, not even I, can tell where he is to be found. You must let your drums resound far and wide, through woods and over plains, drum and sing for hours, for days and for nights calling 'RAIN, RAIN, O RAIN . . .' Drum without pause until the old man Rain hears you and sends you water to spare your pains of thirst."

From that time on, the Indians have been divided into the Sun People and the Moon People, and they sing the rain songs for all the others. They are the rain watchers and rain bringers. But sometimes they wonder: would there be hunger, thirst or drought here on earth had the great-great-grandfathers of their great-great-grandfathers not chased away the Sun, the Moon and the Rain? Who knows for certain? Perhaps the spotted jaguars in the jungle do.